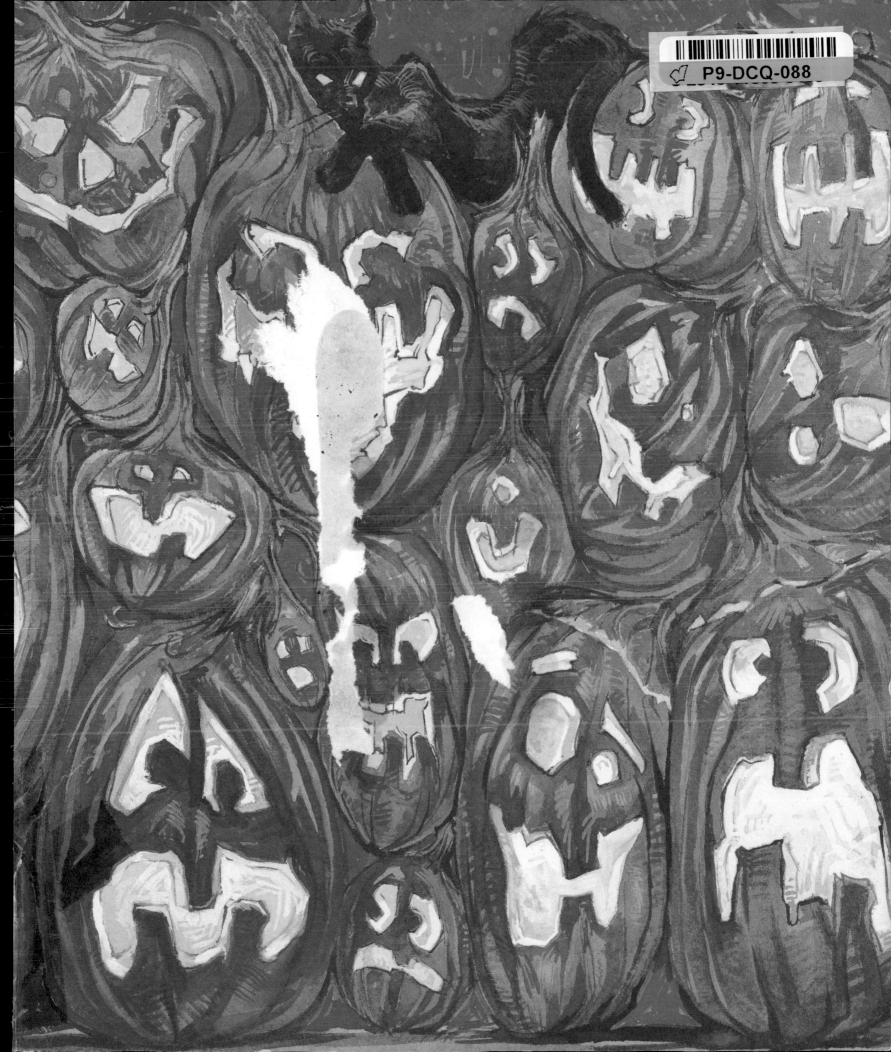

P9-DCQ-088

For my special little monster, Quinn
—D. S.

Dedicated to the memory of dear
Iko Bayarsaikhan, 1992–2007
—M. F.

Published by
PEACHTREE PUBLISHERS
1700 Chattahoochee Avenue
Atlanta, Georgia 30318-2112
www.peachtree-online.com

Text © 2008 by Danny Schnitzlein
Illustrations © 2008 by Matt Faulkner

All rights reserved. No part of this publication may be reproduced,
stored in a retrieval system, or transmitted in any form
or by any means—electronic, mechanical,
photocopy, recording, or any other—
except for brief quotations in printed reviews,
without the prior permission of the publisher.

Art direction by Loraine M. Joyner
Composition by Melanie McMahon Ives
Illustrations created in watercolor on
100% rag archival watercolor paper

Printed in China
10 9 8 7 6 5 4 3 2 1
First Edition

Library of Congress Cataloging-in-Publication Data

Schnitzlein, Danny.
  Trick or treat on Monster Street / written by Danny Schnitzlein ;
illustrated by Matt Faulkner. -- 1st ed.
    p. cm.
  Summary: A boy whose brothers taunt him because of his fears gets
revenge when he finds himself alone on Monster Street on Halloween.
  ISBN 13: 978-1-56145-465-5 / ISBN 10: 1-56145-465-6
  [1. Stories in rhyme. 2. Monsters--Fiction. 3. Fear--Fiction. 4.
Halloween--Fiction. 5. Brothers--Fiction.] 1. Faulkner, Matt, ill. 11.
Title.
  PZ8.3.S2972Tr 2008
  [E]--dc22   2008005000

TRICK OR TREAT
ON
M🐵NSTER
STREET

Written by Danny Schnitzlein
Illustrated by Matt Faulkner

PEACHTREE
ATLANTA

CROMWELL BELDEN PUBLIC LIBRARY
39 WEST STREET
CROMWELL, CT 06416

I used to be a scaredy cat,
   afraid to sleep in my own bed.
Late at night, when things went bump,
   I'd conjure monsters in my head.

My brothers knew my weakness well.
   Every time they got the chance,
      They'd think of ways to make me scream,
      and laugh when I would wet my pants.

But now I've changed. I laugh at ghosts.
Monsters fill me with delight.
It happened, as you might have guessed,
one dark and spooky Halloween night.

A mummy stomped inside my room.
A snarling werewolf marched in too.
"Come on!" my older brothers growled.
"Dad says to trick-or-treat with you!"

I pulled my rabbit costume on.
They laughed like mad when I was done.
"A bunny suit?" my brothers joked.
"That costume won't scare anyone!"

They grabbed my hands and off we ran,
to trick-or-treat from door to door.
When people handed candy out,
my greedy brothers grabbed for more.

We took a shortcut through the woods.
I stopped to tie my tennis shoe.
I stood and found myself alone.
I called out, "Guys?"

An owl said . . ."Who?"

I stumbled blindly through the dark,
and tried to blink away my tears.
Two trees reached out to rip my suit.
Another snatched my bunny ears.

A creature howled out in the night.
A road appeared beneath my feet.

Monster St.

The moon glowed full
and round and bright.
A weathered sign said,
"Monster Street."

Lightning flashed.
  Thunder boomed.
    Freezing rain began to pour.

I sprinted to the nearest house
and pounded on the heavy door.

The deadbolt clicked. The door squeaked open.
Inch by inch, an arm reached out.
I opened up my goody bag.
The arm dropped in a smelly trout!

I fled next door and knocked once more.
That door creaked open just a crack.
A slimy tentacle snaked out
and dropped some spiders in my sack!
I turned around and nearly screamed.
Another kid was standing there.
But something didn't look quite right.
His skin? His eyes? His nose? His hair?

Green fingers gripped his chin and pulled.
His face began to stretch and peel.
The human face was just a mask!
The monster underneath was real!
And when that monster shed his coat,
I got another big surprise.
A larger creature lurked beneath,
    with fangs and horns and
        gruesome eyes!

"My name is Ed," the big guy said. The little one growled, "Call me Gus.
Your costume is the best we've seen. Why don't you trick-or-trout with us?"

I wondered if they'd eat me up when they found out I wore no mask.
I shook their claws and faked a smile. I prayed that they would never ask.

We filled our sacks with squirming snacks.
Gus gobbled down a wriggling snake.
Ed offered me a slug. I said,
"No thanks. I've got a stomachache."

At last we reached the street's dead end. A sign said,
"House of Fear. Beware!"
It looked just like my house back home. I wondered what went on in there.

The house was filled with monster folks, dressed up to look like humans do.
Gus and Ed were terrified. They stuck to me like superglue.
Cuddly little bunnies hopped and playful kittens pranced about.
When barking puppy dogs appeared, my monster friends screamed,

"LET US OUT!"

A squeaky staircase led us down, and on the bottom floor we found
A monster party going on, one hundred feet below the ground.

Mummies rapped and werewolves crooned.
Two vampires did the chicken dance.
And once I think I might have seen
my history teacher Mr. Lance.

"I'm Gertie!" said a monster girl. She pulled me on the floor to dance.
We did the cha-cha and the twist, until I nearly split my pants.

We joked and laughed and sang some songs.
And finally I began to see...

That though we came from
different worlds,
Those monster kids were
just like me.

A cyclops with a microphone said,
"Every vampire, witch, and ghost
Put on your mask. It's time to see
which costume makes us scream the most!"
A drumroll buzzed. The crowd grew hushed.
A spotlight roamed around the place.
And when, at last, it came to rest,
that beam was shining on my face!

The monsters cheered. I took the prize: a heavy squirming sack.

I held my breath and peeked inside.
The thing inside of it looked back!

The monsters formed a big parade and carried me down Monster Street.
Near the woods where I'd come in, they set me down upon my feet.

I heard my brothers yell my name. I said, "I've gotta go. It's late."
I started running toward the woods. My monster buddies yelled out,

"Wait!"

I hung my head. My face turned red, and I began to bawl.
"I'm just a human kid," I sobbed. "I'm not a monster after all."
Then Gertie grinned and laughed out loud. She said, "I knew it all along!
Especially when you didn't know the words to any monster song."

Gus and Ed said, "We weren't fooled,
'cause back there in the House of Fear,
We were running for the door—
you stopped and scratched a puppy's ear."

I told them how my brothers liked
to scare me in the dark of night.
The monsters asked for my address
and then they giggled with delight.

With tearful eyes we said goodbyes.
I'd made new friends that I would miss.
Gertie told me, "Close your eyes."
And then I got a monster kiss!

I opened up my eyes to find my friends had vanished in the air.
"Where have you been?" my brothers yelled.
"We searched and hunted everywhere!"

They snatched away my goody bag and plunged their greedy hands inside.
But when they saw what I'd brought back,
they screamed and wet their pants and cried.

I said good night and doused the light.
I pulled the covers to my chin.
A smile crept across my face.
I knew the fun would soon begin.
Late that night, to my delight,
I heard a scream and then a "GRRRR!"
My brothers claim two monsters came.
Or was it three? They weren't quite sure.

I used to be a scaredy cat, but I sleep soundly in my bed.
And late at night, when things go bump, I think of Gertie, Gus, and Ed.
I've looked again for Monster Street, in battered books, on tattered maps.
I've walked the woods for weeks and weeks. Could it have been a dream?

Perhaps.

But maybe when the moon is full, you'll find that hidden passage through,
And trick-or-treat on Monster Street, where monsters are afraid of you!